BOOK 1

Stewy Baby
Finds A Home

Kristin Cooper-Herby

Illustrations by Blake Coker

Stewy Baby Finds A Home

Bitterroot Mountain
PUBLISHING

9030 N Hess #331,
Hayden, ID 83835

Illustrations by Blake Coker
Interior Design by Jera Publishing
Editing by Fallon Abolafia

Paperback ISBN: 978-1-940025-20-9
E-Book ISBN: 978-1-940025-21-6

To Stewy Baby
I will always love you.

Contents

Pick of the Litter

MY MOM NUDGED me out of my blissful sleep. "You were whimpering in your sleep again, little one. Were you dreaming about the girl?"

I had been dreaming about the girl. The happy little girl with red braids; she was super sparkly, and missing her two front teeth. Whenever I had this dream, I smelled something sweet, and delicious, and I always woke up hungry.

"She seems so real, Mama. What does it mean?"

"I'm not sure, but I think she might be your special human. You're lucky to have that vision little one." My mom assured me.

"What if my special human doesn't look like the girl in my dreams? How will I know it's her?"

"You'll know, little one, you can feel it in your bones. You need to impress her, and make her want you."

"How do I do that Mama?" I asked.

"You look her in the eye, and give her a big kiss. Then you wag your tail."

"But I don't have a tail." I replied confused.

"Then wag your nub." Mama laughed.

I was born in a big red barn on a rainy day in July. I had three sisters and four brothers. Seven of us were born with tails and one was born without. I was the unfortunate one that was born without. I had a nub, but nubs didn't count. I was the plainest puppy of the litter, not to mention I had a really bad case of the wind ever since I was put on puppy chow. The stuff just didn't agree with me. My Mom said I was the pick of the litter, but I didn't feel that way.

"You're beautiful in your own special way. You're smart, and you have a wonderful personality." My Mom assured me.

"When will she come? When will someone choose me?" I whined. All of my other siblings had been adopted.

"Be patient little one, it will happen."

But would it happen? I loved my canine Mom, but I longed for a human family of my own. I longed for the girl.

My Mom, Lucky, is the smartest dog ever. She's an Australian Shepherd with black fur and fabulous tan markings on her face and legs. My Father is a Corgi, but I have never met him. He loved my Mother very much, but his human family moved shortly before I was born.

The next day I was in the barn playing chase with Bubba, the barn mouse, when I stopped in my tracks. I smelled something familiar and delicious.

In the sunlight of the big red barn stood a lady and two small humans; a boy and a girl. The boy was taller than the girl and wore a piece of cloth tied around his neck, and a cowboy hat. The little girl wore a puffy bright thing around her waist, and sparkling shoes. She had red hair and braids. She looked and smelled like my dream. The girl and I locked eyes. Our eyes were the same color of blue. She gave me a big goofy smile. She was missing her two front teeth. I felt my knees begin to shake. Was this what my Mom meant? Was I feeling it in my bones?

"This is the last pup we have left." Laura, my Mom's human said pointing to me. "I must say I've grown very fond of her. She's a smart one. It's almost as if she understands humans."

I do understand humans. My Mom says it's my special gift. I have been trying to keep it a secret, but I think Laura is on to me. Ever since I was born, I could understand the human language. My Mom Lucky understands it too and she has been teaching me all of the words that she knows. I may have been the only pup born without a tail, but I was also the only pup that could understand humans. I wish I could speak the human language, but my Mom says that's impossible, and to be thankful for the gift that I have.

The little girl and I ran towards each other. As I got closer, the sweet smell got stronger and stronger. She fell to the ground, and I licked her hands and then her face. She tasted delicious!

"She's the one I've been dreaming about, Mommy; see how much she loves me?" The girl said.

"She loves your pancakes and syrup," her brother grumped. "I told you to wipe your face."

Pancakes and syrup were delicious. I wanted to eat it every day!

"Katie, remember we're just looking today. We can't take her until Daddy builds a fence." The Mommy said.

"Yeah Katie, Dad wouldn't be very happy if we picked out a dog without him."

What? They were just looking? But this little girl was my human. They had to take me home.

"That's a shame you can't take her today, I have another family coming by to look at her in about an hour. They sounded very interested." Laura said.

Thank you Laura! I thought.

"No, Mommy she can't go to another family, she's meant to be with us, she wants to go home with us." Katie cried.

"Katie, calm down. Maybe we can work something out. Come here honey; let's take a look at you." The Mom cooed to me.

I waddled over to them wagging my nub. I plunked down between the Mom and the boy. I licked one, and then the other. They both laughed.

"This is my Mom, Kristi, and my dumb brother Cooper. I'm Katie. Tell them how much you want to come home with us."

I turned to Cooper and Kristi, cocked my head from side to side and barked.

"Geez Kate, it's not like the dog talks, or understands you," the dumb brother, Cooper said.

"She does so understand me, Coop, she barked at you didn't she? She has special powers just like me," Katie said crossing her arms and then looking at her Mom. "We have to take her Mommy; she's the one I've been telling you about."

"What's all this about special powers?" Laura asked.

"Sometimes Katie sees things in her dreams that happen in the future. Lately, she's been dreaming about a little puppy that looks like a spotted bear cub. She described her to me just this morning; she said she's grey, black and white, with tan eyebrows and a little tail. She also said she lives in a big red barn. We were on our way home from dance class, when Katie saw the barn, and insisted that we stop."

"Wow, that's really strange. It's almost like it was meant to be." Laura said.

"It was meant to be, she's the special dog I've been dreaming about. She's different, just like me. She doesn't have a tail, and I have red hair. But different can be beautiful!" Katie said.

"How old are you?" Laura asked.

"I'm six, but my Mom says I'm wise beyond my years."

"She sucks at math," dummy brother, Cooper said.

"Don't we all." Laura laughed.

"We have to take her today Mommy; it can be a surprise for Daddy." Katie pleaded.

I held my breath. Please say yes, please say yes. I repeated to myself. Kristi furrowed her eyebrows deep in thought.

"So where did her tail go? Did you chop it off?" Cooper asked Laura.

"No, we didn't chop it off. She was born without a tail. Her Mom, Lucky had eight puppies, seven had tails, and this pup didn't." Laura said.

"That's cool, but I really wanted a boy dog. She sort of looks like a boy, are you sure she's not?"

"I'm afraid this one's definitely a little girl, but she is kind of a Tomboy. Is that good enough?"

"Coop, I told you, Spud is a boy, so we need a girl to even things out." Katie said.

Spud? Who the heck was this Spud guy? Another dog? Another human? Please tell me he wasn't a cat. I do not like cats.

I knew I had to win Cooper over, so I ran over to him and licked and licked his face until he fell over backwards with laughter.

"Okay, okay," Cooper said. "I like her, but if we keep her, you can't dress her up in tutus, Katie."

"Why not, I think she would look cute in tutus, wouldn't you?" Katie asked me.

I glanced at my Mom Lucky. She gave me an approving canine smile. I could tell she liked this human family as much as I did.

"Dogs don't wear tutus Katie, especially dogs that look like boys." Cooper said.

Why was everyone saying I looked like a boy? I didn't look like a boy, I was clearly a girl.

"So you could always surprise your husband and give him this pup as a gift." Laura said to Kristi.

"Yeah, I suppose we could put a big bow on her, and give him an early birthday present." Kristi said.

"A big, pink bow! Daddy will be so surprised," yelled Katie.

"Oh, Daddy will be surprised alright," Cooper remarked.

"Surprised in a good way right?" Laura said.

"Right, Daddy loves dogs." Katie said dancing circles around me.

"Daddy does love dogs. Don't worry about my husband, Laura, he wanted to wait until we had a fence built, but this will just speed up the process." Kristi said picking me up. "I wouldn't be taking this cute little bear cub if I didn't think this would work out for all of us." She gave me a gentle squeeze.

Just then it happened. I couldn't hold it in anymore. The little love squeeze did it – my gas escaped me. Cooper was the first to notice.

"Gross, what's that smell?"

"Pee yew. Coop, did you fart?" Katie asked plugging her nose.

I was devastated. I had come so close this time. The deal was almost done and I had to ruin it with my gas.

"I'm afraid this little puppy has a bad case of the wind." Laura said.

"C o o o o o o o o o o o l ." C o o p e r said, grinning.

Had my gas won Cooper over?

"Sometimes it takes them awhile to adjust to their puppy food. It should pass in a few days."

"She's not sick is she?" Kristi asked.

"No, she's as healthy as a horse. She's just a gassy little thing."

I was horrified. Not only had I stunk up the whole barn, but they were talking about my gas and comparing me to a horse? This family was never going to take me. I would live in the barn forever. Katie was going to be heart broken.

Kristi held me away from her and looked at me. "A little gas never hurt anything. You kind of smell like my brother Kevin. We'll see if we can find some puppy food that agrees with you, okay?"

Did this mean they were keeping me? They really didn't care about my stinky gas? What did Katie call it? A fart? That was a new human word for me.

"So we can keep her?" Cooper asked.

"I thought you didn't want a girl dog, Cooper." Katie said.

"I didn't, but a girl dog that farts is way cool."

"Yes, we can keep her," Kristi said lovingly petting my head.

"Hooray, hooray! I finally found my

special dog. I told you she was in this barn!" Katie cheered.

My heart did a joyful flip. My puppy dream had finally come true. I had found my little red head girl and a family that loved me just the way I was.

"Go say goodbye to your mama, Baby Girl." Kristi said to me gently placing me on the ground.

I slowly started walking over to my Mom.

"See, I told you she understands humans." Katie said.

I had forgotten that by finding my special humans, I would have to leave my Mom. I felt sad inside, and my eyes started to tear up. I licked my Mama's paws and then her nose. I looked at her and whimpered. She put her paw on my head squashing me to the ground. She looked me directly in the eyes and whined. She was telling me this was my future, this, was my new beginning. She had done her duty in raising me and now it was up to me. I gave her one last nuzzle and turned to my new human family.

Katie scooped me up in her arms and gave me a big hug. "Let's go home Baby Girl!"

CHAPTER 2

The Pink Palace

"THIS IS A CAR," Katie explained as she placed me in a small metal box with wheels. I had never been in a car before. I had seen the ranch hands drive a tractor but I had never seen a car.

"Katie, you can't hog her just because you said you dreamed about her, I want her to sit on my lap," Cooper said.

"No, my lap!" Katie yelled.

"Guys, don't argue. She can sit right here in the middle of both of you." Kristi placed me in the backseat between the kids. I wasn't sure I wanted to be in this boxy thing. I felt like I couldn't breathe. This car was hotter than the barn on a summer day.

"Mom, unroll the windows, it's soooooo hot in here." Cooper said.

"Yeah Mom, you're freaking our dog out. What are you trying to do cook us like a hotdog?" Katie giggled. "Get it, a HOT DOG?"

"Very funny, Kate." Cooper said.

"Sorry guys, I don't want to unroll the windows, I'm afraid the puppy will try to jump out," Kristi remarked. "I'll just crack the windows a bit, until the air conditioning kicks in."

Just then we started moving. What the heck was this thing? I jumped on Cooper's lap and tried to put my head outside, but my wet nose smashed into something clear.

"Gross, she just smashed her nose into the window. Check out the snotty smudge she left." Cooper laughed.

"Cooper, she's confused. Come here baby." Katie grabbed me from Cooper. "These are just windows. It looks like you're outside but you're not." Katie knocked on the window with her small fist. "You're riding in a car. It gets us from one place to another. You don't have anything to worry about. Just close your eyes and fall asleep. We'll be home in no time."

I was so glad that Katie explained that to me. I felt much better. I curled up between my new humans and fell asleep to the lull of the movement. This was a big day.

I woke up when the car stopped. I don't know how long I was asleep.

"We're home Baby Girl." Katie whispered, gently carrying me out of the car. She set me inside the house on a big pink softness that went on forever. Humans always think that dogs are color blind. They think we only see black, white and gray. The truth is, we see colors even brighter than humans do. My old house was a red barn with brown dirt floors. Every now and then we were able to go onto the bright green grass and run around. This house was something completely different. I wasn't even sure what color this was. The ground was much softer than the dirt floor of the barn. My puppy paws sunk into the brightness. I was afraid to walk. I was afraid I would sink into the pool of color.

"It's okay baby girl, this is called carpet. I guess you haven't ever been on carpet before, have you?" Katie asked.

I looked at her and cocked my head to one side then looked down at the carpet and barked as I pawed it.

"I know. It's kind of pink isn't it? I'm afraid I went a little crazy when Dan and I got married. Everything had to be pink including my house…. Do you even see pink?" Kristi asked.

I cocked my head and barked.

"She does see pink! Good thing we didn't get a boy dog right?" Katie said.

"I think she hates pink just like I do." Cooper said as he stroked my head.

"Pink is a beautiful color Cooper, isn't that right Baby Girl?" Katie said.

"Her name isn't Baby Girl Katie. I think I should get to name her since you picked her out."

"No, I want to name her. I think she should have a princess name."

"No, I think she should have a cowboy name since she was born on a farm." Cooper argued.

"She's not a cow or a boy, dummy." Katie shouted.

"Mooooom, Katie called me dummy!" Cooper yelled.

"That's enough guys." Kristi said. "You know I don't care for the word hate or dummy. This is a new place for our puppy and we want to make her feel welcome. Yelling at each other won't make her feel happy will it?"

"Sorry." The kids muttered.

"Okay, let's show our new puppy around our house." Kristi said.

I barked at them and wagged my nub then started exploring this big pink house. Kristi was right; she did go crazy with PINK. Almost everything in this house was pink, including the things that spun around on the ceiling. The only room that wasn't pink was Cooper's room. It had horses and cowboys all over the place. I knew, because I was born on a farm.

"You two play nice with our puppy, while I go call Mimi and tell her all about our new addition to the family."

Kristi picked up the phone and dialed.

"Hi Mom, I have exciting news! "Kristi said. "Remember I told you about the dream Katie had been having about the little puppy that looked like a spotted bear cub? Well, we were driving home from Katie's dance class today and she insisted we stop at this big red barn. She said that's where the puppy lives that she had been dreaming about…Yes, she did live there and we brought her home."

I had wandered into the kitchen to listen to Kristi's conversation. The kids were in Cooper's cowboy room on the top bunk bed trying to figure out my name.

"Come over tomorrow and see her, she wants to meet her Grandma…. I love you too Mom! … Okay, see you tomorrow."

Kristi looked at me and said, "That was your Grandma, Baby Girl! She wants to come meet you."

Just then the kids ran downstairs yelling at the top of their lungs that they had decided on a name for me. Boy was I happy. I was getting a little tired of being called Baby Girl, and puppy.

"Mommy, Mommy, Coop and I figured out the perfect name for our new puppy," Katie yelled.

"Yep, Katie said I could pick her first name since she got to get a girl." Cooper said.

"That's great guys, what did you two come up with?" Kristi asked.

Yeah guys, what did you come up with? I wondered. I couldn't wait to hear my new name. The name I would have for the rest of my life, the name I would come running to at any command. A real dog name!

"Stewart!" Cooper exclaimed jumping up and down.

"Stewart?" Kristi asked surprised.

"Stewart?" I thought. I had envisioned a pretty name like Daisy or Diamond. Not a boy name like Stewart.

"Yes, Stewart!" Katie said. "Actually, it's Stewart- Duke Anna-Belle Campbell. Coop thought Stewart Duke sounded like a cowboy name and I added the middle name. We let you and Daddy pick the last name."

"But Daddy and I didn't choose the last name," Kristi said.

"Silly Mommy, yes you did." Katie said.

"Yeah," Cooper said. "That's our families' last name. You and Daddy picked it."

"Okay, well, I guess Stewart-Duke Anna-Belle Campbell it is." Kristi said.

"But I'm gonna call her Anna-Belle 'cause Stewart is a boy name." Katie said.

"Let's try to agree on one name to call her while we're training her, so she doesn't get confused. What do you think about Stewy?" Kristi asked the kids.

"I like Stewy." Cooper said.

"How about Stewy Baby?" Katie asked.

"I like Stewy Baby." Kristi said.

"What do you think Stewy Baby? Does that sound like a good name to you?" Katie asked me.

I tilted my head from side to side and thought about it. I really liked the name Jewel, but as long as all of my humans were happy, I was good with that. I looked at them and barked and then I spun around in a circle.

"She likes it, she like it!" The kids screamed, jumping up and down. My family of humans joined hands and danced around me in a circle singing "Stewy Baby, Stewy Baby!" Then they all fell to the ground and laughed. I waddled over and graced all of their faces with my kisses and puppy breath.

Stewy Baby it was!

When it was time for bed, Kristi put me on top of her warm pink bed. "Slumber party," she sang to the kids. The kids jumped on the bed and laughed.

"Can we all sleep with you tonight Mommy?" Katie said with her goofy smile.

"Even Stewy Baby?" Cooper asked.

"Yes, we can all sleep together tonight." Kristi said.

"That's good, because Stewy's sad. She misses her real Mama." Katie said.

I thought of Lucky, my canine Mom at home alone in the barn. I wondered if she was feeling lonely. I missed her a lot, but I was also happy with my new humans.

Cooper nudged my bottom with his hand so that I snuggled up to all of them.

"Let's sing Stewy the Get-Along- Song!" Kristi said.

"Good idea, Mommy!" Katie said.

"Get a long Stewy Baby,

Sing my song Stewy Baby,

It goes la la la la la la la,

La la la la la

La… la la la laaaaaaaaaaaa." Katie sang in a sweet voice slightly off key.

"You are mine, Stewy Baby,

Always shine, Stewy Baby,

And we'll sing and dance and run and jump,

I'll love you all the time,

I'm… so glad you're mine." Katie continued.

"Go to sleep, Stewy Baby,

Please don't weep, Stewy Baby,

Close your eyes and have sweet dreams of our

Fun upcoming days,

Fun… in so many ways." Kristi sang in a soft soothing voice.

"Get along, Stewy Baby,

Sing my song, Stewy Baby,

It goes la la la la la la la

La la la la la,

La…… la la la laaaaaaaaaaaa." Cooper sang.

By the time they finished the song, I was fast asleep.

CHAPTER 3

Spud

I WOKE UP the next morning a bit dazed and confused. I had crazy dreams the night before about pink fans, a Mom, a cowboy and a princess in a big cozy pink bed. I opened my eyes and saw what else? PINK! Then I remembered. It wasn't a dream. I had found my humans and they had brought me to a wonderful pink palace where I didn't have to sleep on a hard brown surface anymore. Kristi had actually let me come into her big pink bed and sleep with her and the kids, all night long!

"Just this once, so you won't miss your Mama." Kristi had said. "Believe me; this won't be happening once Dan gets home."

I had slept in between them all night; I got up and waddled over to Katie: she was still sleeping. I gave her a big sloppy puppy kiss right on her cheek. She giggled. I licked her again. She opened her eyes.

"Ohhhhhhh, good morning, Baby Girl," Katie whispered. "I couldn't figure out who was giving me warm kisses and then I remembered. I have my new Stewy Baby! Did you sleep well?"

I barked once.

"Shhhhhhhhhh." Katie whispered looking at her Mom and Cooper. "Let's let them sleep a little bit longer. You probably have to go potty don't you?"

I barked quietly and wagged my nub.

"You are the smartest doggy ever!" Katie gave me a kiss on the tip of my wet nose and jumped out of bed. She opened the bedroom door and we started racing down the stairs. I came to a screeching halt halfway down. A big fluffy, black and grey striped barn cat was waiting at the bottom of the stairs giving me the stink eye. What in the world was a barn cat doing in the pink palace?

I looked at Katie and barked and then looked back at the stink-eyed cat.

"Oh, there you are Spuddy boy!" Katie said. "I thought you were outside. You haven't met Stewy Baby yet."

Spud glared at both of us.

"Don't look at us that way! This is your new sister, Stewy Baby. Stewy Baby, this is Spud the cat."

Katie looked at me lovingly and coaxed, "It's okay Stewy, Spud won't hurt you. Will you Spud? Go say hi."

She nudged my bottom towards Spud. I tentatively walked down the remaining stairs and sniffed him slowly. He didn't smell nearly as bad as the barn cats. Spud sniffed me back and I stayed very still.

My canine mom Lucky had warned me about getting too close to the barn cats. "They're filthy creatures. One swipe of the claw and you get an infection that only a doctor can fix!" Lucky had said.

Spud sniffed my bottom (a little too close for my liking) then sniffed my face. I gave a quizzical look thinking that maybe we could be friends. I barked at him to say

hello. Spud jumped straight up into the air, hissed at me, then wacked my face with his left paw.

"Yipe, yipe, yipe." I yelped and ran back behind Katie.

"Spud," Katie yelled. "That was not nice! That is not how we welcome someone into our family!"

I peeked between Katie's legs and saw Spud give me a look of disgust. He looked at Katie long and hard as if to say "Why did you have to go and ruin my life?"

"Oh Spud, you'll be fine!" Katie said as she patted him. "You got used to me and Coop, you'll get used to Stewy Baby too. Besides, you'll always be my favorite kitty. There's enough love in this house for a cat and a dog!"

Obviously, Spud did not agree. He fluffed his tail up, gave us both one last glare, then turned and walked away.

CHAPTER 4

Human Grandparents

"WHERE ARE MY GRANDKIDS and their new puppy?" A high pitch voice screeched.

"Mimi!" The kids exclaimed.

I had been upstairs with the kids playing dress up. Katie was dressed as a princess ballerina and Cooper was dressed as a cowboy with a cape. I had seen a lot of cowboys on the farm but none of them had ever worn what Cooper called his "Super Cape." Katie was just attempting to put a dress on me when the loud voice came echoing up the stairs.

"We're upstairs Mimi." Katie yelled down.

Up the stairs bounded the most energetic human I had ever seen.

"Ohhhhh look at how cute you are! You do look like a little bear cub." The crazy lady kneeled down and talked right into my face. "Who's the good puppy? Who loves their Grandma?"

"Mimi, you're freaking her out. She's doesn't like humans to get that close to her face. Besides, you have garlic-o breath, and Stewy Baby doesn't like garlic-o." Katie said.

"Well, I'm not just any human I'm her Grandma." She looked at me and said, "You can call me Mimi, just like the kids call me Mimi."

I liked this Mimi. I didn't mind her garlic-o breath at all. In fact, it kind of reminded me of the smell in the barn. I barked at Mimi and I barked at Katie to let her know I approved.

"I think she likes you Mimi." Cooper said.

"Of course she likes me, I'm her Mimi. Aren't I your Mimi?" Mimi picked me up and I barked and licked her face. "So Kate, your Mom tells me this is the puppy you were dreaming about."

"Yep, she's the one." Katie said with indifference as she attempted to stick a pink bow to my head. "Look Mimi, she loves pink just like me and Mommy."

"She does, does she? What do you think, Super Cooper?"

"I think she hates pink just like me and Daddy." Cooper said.

"She doesn't hate pink Coop, she's a girl, and girls love pink." Katie argued.

"To tell you the truth, Katie bug, I'm not crazy about pink either." Mimi said.

"See Katie, I told you!" Cooper said. "Just because you're a girl doesn't mean you like pink!" He jumped off the top of his bunk bed, and zoomed around the room in his cape yelling "yee haw!"

"He's one confused boy. He doesn't know if he wants to be a cowboy or a super hero, so he's both. " Kristi said entering Katie's room.

"I'm Super Cooper, the strongest, fastest super cowboy ever." Cooper whooped.

"See what I mean?" Kristi asked Mimi.

"Hmmmmmmm." Mimi mumbled, not really listening to Kristi's Super hero mumbo jumbo. "Tommmmmmm, come upstairs and meet your new Granddog," Mimi yelled down the stairs.

"I'm trying to get the score of the football game. Bring him downstairs," The man voice called.

"Papa Tom!" Cooper called.

"I didn't know Dad came too," said Kristi.

"Let me have her, Mimi, I want to show her to Papa." Cooper grabbed me out of Mimi's hands and ran down the stairs.

"Look Papa Tom, check out our new puppy. Her name is Stewart-Duke Anna-Belle Campbell!" Cooper pushed me towards Papa Tom.

"What's the matter with his eyes?" Papa Tom asked as he inspected me over his glasses.

"What do you mean? SHE has beautiful eyes." Katie said.

"They look like goat eyes." Papa Tom said.

Why, I had never been so insulted in my whole eight week puppy life. Many people had said I wasn't cute, and one had even called me ugly, but comparing me to a goat? They had been the most annoying animals on the farm. Always getting into things they shouldn't be getting into, and pooping whenever and wherever they felt like it. Not to mention their horribly loud voices. They had scary eyes. I didn't like the farm goats and I wasn't sure I liked Papa Tom.

"She does not have goat eyes! She has beautiful eyes. I love her just the way she is." Katie said stroking my head. I ran over to Papa Tom, barked at him and then ran back to hide behind Katie. Papa Tom let out the biggest cackle laugh I had ever heard.

"It looks like she knows who her family is. Hopefully your daddy will like her as much as you all do."

"Look Papa, she doesn't have a tail, isn't that the silliest thing you ever saw on a dog?" Cooper asked.

Papa Tom kneeled down and looked directly at my butt. He lifted my nub and let loose another big belly laugh. I did not like this horse toothed, cackling man. I put my head down and sulked over to Kristi and Katie.

"Papa, you hurt her feelings," Katie scolded. "It's not her fault she was born without a tail."

"Yeah Dad, first you said she has goat eyes and now you're laughing at her nub. That's part of the reason I wanted her. Tails are over-rated; they only get in the way.

We love you just the way you are," Kristi said to me.

"She is very unique looking... She's kind of a Tom boy." Papa Tom said.

That was it. I was done with Papa Tom. I ran over to him, sat at his feet and gave him a piece of my mind. I showed him my teeth and yapped at him. Then, I turned around and shook my nub at him.

"See Daddy will love her just as much as we do!" Katie laughed.

CHAPTER 5

Dan the Man

"HONEY, I'M HOME!" a strange voice boomed up the stairs early the next morning.

"Oh shoot, Dan's home early," Kristi mumbled. "Baby Girl, I need you to stay in this room with the kids and not make a peep." Kristi closed the door. I heard her trot down the pink stairs. I was hoping she wouldn't be long, I had to go potty.

"Hi babe, surprised to see me?" The strange voice said.

"Yeah…. I thought you weren't coming home until this evening," Kristi responded.

"I missed you and the kids, so I decided to drive straight home."

"All the way from California? You're crazy, that's like a 26 hour drive." Kristi said in a high pitched voice.

Kristi sounded weird. She always talked to me in a high pitched voice but it was a happy voice. This one was a nervous voice.

"What's up with you? I thought you would be happy to see me. Where are my kids? Are they still sleeping? " Dan said.

"I am happy to see you… I'm just a little surprised. Yes, the kids are still sleeping so be quiet. I kept them up late last night… we have a surprise for you. We were hoping to have a little more time to prepare it."

"Uh Oh. I don't always like your surprises. They usually cost me money." Dan said.

"Well, I will have you know that this one only cost you $20.00."

That was it. I had enough. I was only eight weeks old after all, and I had held

my pee for as long as I could. I barked and yipped.

"What was that?" Dan asked.

"Ummmm… your surprise." I heard two sets of footsteps coming up the pink stairs which meant I was going to meet this strange man voice.

"Kristi! What in the heck have you done?" Dan exclaimed as he opened the door and saw me.

"Surprise!" Kristi picked me up.

"Daddy, you ruined your surprise…" Katie said, rubbing the sleep out of her eyes and getting out of bed.

"You're kidding me right? You didn't go out and get a dog before we built a fence?" Dan asked Kristi.

"But Daddy, she's the doggy I saw in my dream," Katie whispered as she stroked my neck. I loved it when she did that! I gave a little bark to show her that I was on her side.

"I told you he wouldn't be very happy about it," Cooper said yawning.

"Listen guys, you can't just go out and get a dog whenever you feel like it. I told you it wasn't a good time. We don't have a fence or a kennel or anything else that's dogly!" The Daddy said.

"Silly Daddy, dogly isn't a word," Katie laughed as she hugged her Daddy.

"She's pretty cool, Dad. She's really smart, and we went to the pet store and bought her everything she needs including a kennel." Cooper said.

Dan smiled a little then put on his tough guy act again. He reminded me of my brother Buster. He was always trying to appear tougher and bigger then he was. I was hoping that Dan would be an easier nut to crack than Buster. Just when Buster and I became friends he was bought by some toothless wonder.

"He is very cute, but I don't know that he's staying."

"Daddy, she's a girl, and she has to stay," Katie pleaded. "She's the special one that was meant to be with our family."

"He's really cute Katie Bug, but we're just not ready for a dog yet," Dan said. "Kristi, why do you do this? Why do you buy things while I'm gone?"

"I'm a woman. Women shop." Kristi said.

"Women shop for clothes and household items, not dogs and cars."

I barked and barked and barked! I still had to pee and now something else was starting to brew in my tummy. I had never waited this long to go to the bathroom but my gut told me that it wouldn't be right to go potty on the pink fuzzy carpet.

"What's wrong with him?" asked Dan.

"Her. She probably has to go to the bathroom. She hasn't gone since last night."

"Well put him outside. The last thing we need is for him to have an accident on our carpet."

"Her!" Katie yelled. "Okay. Come on Stewy girl. Let's go potty."

I trotted as fast as I could to keep up with my human so I could make it to the door. I didn't want Dan to get angrier with me. Katie opened the back slider and I ran to the bright green grass and relieved myself.

"Good girl!" Katie said as she picked me up and gave me a big kiss. "See how smart she is Daddy? I picked the smartest one. I haven't even had her for 48 hours and she told me she needed to go potty! Now go poop for me." Katie put me down and I proceeded to squat and do my second duty or should I say doody?

"Good girl! You poop on demand! See daddy? She's the smartest dog around!" Katie was jumping up and down and running circles around my poop. I guess I did something good. Dan was smiling.

"Well I'll be darned," Dan said scratching his head "You did pick a good one Katie bug."

"What's going on out here?" Kristi asked. She and Cooper came and joined

us in the backyard. Cooper was wearing super hero pajamas and his cowboy boots.

"Well, it seems that this is one smart puppy dog. Katie just told her to go poop, and she did!"

"Yeah, she understands Katie. I didn't believe her at first but she really does. Maybe it's because Katie dreamed about her." Cooper said.

Kristi and Dan shot one another a look. Kristi was peering at Dan with an "I told you so" look on her face.

"Well, Coop. I have to say I was a little surprised. I wish you guys would have waited until I had built a fence." Dan said.

"But she was my special doggy, Daddy. I couldn't let another family take her." Katie said kneeling beside me. "We were meant to be her special family right Mommy?"

"That's right Katie, we were all meant to be one big happy family, right Dan?" Kristi glanced sideways at Dan.

"Riggggggggggght." Dan sighed.

"So we can keep her? We can keep her?" Katie asked jumping up and down.

"We'll see," Dan replied.

"Yippee." Cooper said pretending to shoot the sky.

"I said, we'll see. I'm still not happy about this. Let's give it a week and see how it goes."

"The two of you need a proper introduction. Stewy Baby, this is Dan. Dan, meet Stewart-Duke Anna-Belle Campbell." Kristi shoved me at Dan.

"Me and Coop picked the name Daddy." Katie said.

"Coop and I." Cooper corrected Katie.

"Hello Stewart! It's a good thing you could poop on demand, if you would have had an accident on my carpet, you would have been out today," Dan said as he stroked my head. A little too rough for my liking, just like Buster but I had taught

Buster a thing or two about being gentle and almost human; perhaps I could help Dan as well.

CHAPTER 6

Jail Break

"SO SMART GAL, what are you going to do with Stewart today while we're at work and the kids are at school?" Dan the Man asked Kristi.

"We're taking her to show and tell, right Coop?" Katie piped in.

Show and what? I wasn't sure what this was and I wasn't sure I wanted to know. It sounded scary.

"Yep, she's coming to school with us today," Cooper told his Dad.

"No guys, she's not going to school with you today. We need to ask your teachers first."

"Awwww Mom, we want to show her to our friends," Cooper whined.

"She's going to either stay inside in her kennel or stay outside." Kristi informed everyone.

"I think Stewy would rather stay outside." said Katie. "If I were a dog, I would want to stay outside and not in a kennel. Besides, maybe she'll make a new friend today."

That was the great thing about Katie. She was always trying to put herself in my shoes, or should I say my paws? I'm thinking that maybe she was a dog in a prior life because she always knows what I want.

"If we had a fence that would be a great plan but we don't," Dan the Man said.

"Don't worry Dad. Mom and I rigged up a really cool contraption; it's a leash that screws into the ground so Stewy can't run away." Cooper said.

"Sounds like an accident waiting to happen. This is your deal guys, I'm going to work." Dan gave me a small pat on the head, kissed Kristi and the kids and walked out the door.

"A lot of help he is! Okay, guys, let's get Stewy's bed and water and put it outside." Kristi said to the kids as she opened the slider to the backyard.

Katie followed behind carrying my pink bed while Cooper carried my water dish and a treat. Cooper always snuck me treats, it was great.

"Coop, don't give Stewy that treat, I think that's what's been giving her gas." Kristi said as Cooper tossed the treat into my drooling chops.

"I like it when she has gas," Coop laughed "especially when it's loud and stinky."

"Boys are so gross, aren't they Stewy Baby?" Katie kneeled down in front of me and gently caressed my neck. "We have to go to school now Stewy, but we won't be gone for long. You can take a nice, long nap under our big pine tree and we'll play dress up when I get home okay?"

I barked at Katie to let her know I understood. Everyone thinks that dogs don't know what humans are saying. It's true that most cute, pure bred dogs like poodles or Cocker Spaniels have no idea what their humans are saying. BLAH, BLAH, BLAH is what it sounds like to purebred dogs. Their breeders got too greedy and tried to make them beautiful to sell them for more money, but more money means less brains. That's why I'm so smart. I'm no looker but I can understand even the dumbest human. Kristi and Katie saw it right away. Pretty isn't always better!

"Don't worry Stewy, I won't make you play dress up again. We can play ball okay?" Coop said.

Dress up, or fetch? What a dilemma. I really didn't mind it so much when Katie put her pink tutus on me, but she really needed to figure out that I can't wear human shoes. She tries to shove these pink plastic things on my feet and it just doesn't work.

"Okay Stewy, come here and we'll hook you up to your leash." Kristi said.

I walked over to Kristi and she attached my collar to a long leash that was screwed into the ground. I had watched Kristi and Cooper screw that thing into the ground earlier in the morning but I had no idea I would be attached to it. I didn't like being attached to this thing. I chewed on it to see if I could break free.

"I don't think she likes it." Katie said.

"She'll be okay; it's just for a little bit." Kristi said with an unsure look. "I don't have the heart to leave her in the kennel all day."

"I don't think we should leave her Mom." Cooper said.

"Unfortunately Coop, we don't have a choice. She has her bed, and water, and the shade of this big pine tree. We'll be home in no time Stewy, I promise." Kristi assured me.

They all showered me with hugs and kisses and walked back into the house.

Silence.

I didn't like silence. I barked, I yelped, and I whined. Nothing, I was stuck to the ground. I could walk a ways, but not far. This was horrible. What in the world were Kristi and Cooper thinking?!

A black and white bird flew to the tree beside me and landed on a branch. He started laughing at me. "Caw, Caw. Ya stupid dog. Why did ya let that lady tie ya to that stake? Don't ever trust a human. They'll try to squash your personality and mold you into a dumb pet."

I glanced up at the nasty bird and said, "You don't know what you're talking about you nasty bird! My humans would never do anything like that to me."

"Don't cha know, that cha don't need a human? Look at me. I don't have a human and I'm free to fly around and do whatever I want to do. Humans are overrated." The bird squawked.

"I love my humans." I said.

"Yeah, we'll see how much ya love your humans in a few hours when you're still here, and you're hot, thirsty and miserable."

"They won't leave me here for long; they'll be back in no time!" I said to the nasty squawking bird.

"We'll see, we'll see." The annoying bird said as he swooped over my head, brushing me with his long tail feathers.

Silence again. I think I would rather be taunted by the nasty bird. I lay down in my pink bed and tried to make the best of my time. I was beginning to get scared. Had they forgotten me? I dozed off for a while before I awoke to the screeching bird.

"Caw, Caw. I told ya so, I told ya so." The bird laughed.

"How long have I been here?" I asked.

"About three hundred and seventy hours." The bird responded.

"Three hundred and seventy hours? Kristi said I would only be alone for a short time." I was confused.

"In bird hours."

"Bird hours? What are bird hours?"

"You've heard of dog years, right? They're different than human years and bird hours are different than dog hours, and human hours. Name's Ed, by the way"

"Hi Ed, I'm Stewy. My canine Mom Lucky told me to never trust a crow," I said.

"I'm not a crow, I'm a magpie, the crow's my cousin. We're much better than crows."

"What makes you better?" I asked

"Well, for one thing, we are black AND white. When the sun hits our feathers just right, the black appears to be a dazzlin' bluish purple. For another thing, we have magnificently long tails, not just short nubby tails like the crow... no offense."

"My humans like my nub." I said.

"Yeah, they would. Last of all, we only eat good garbage, from middle class families. No siree Bob, no dump yards and bad neighborhoods for us magpies." Ed said.

"Garbage isn't good for you."

"Yeah well, don't knock it until you've tried it. It just so happens that today is my favorite day of the week, garbage day. What say I help ya get out of this crazy contraption and we have ourselves a little neighborhood buffet?"

"Really? You would do that for me? It is getting very hot out here. I just don't want to disappoint my humans."

"Your humans will think you are that much smarter. You'll make them proud." Ed said.

"Okay. Tell me what to do." I said reluctantly.

"Dig man, dig!"

"For your information, I'm a girl. Do you really think a boy would have a pink collar and a pink bed?"

"Yeah, yeah, whatever," Ed pointed his beak at the stake, "just take your paws, and dig at that screwy thing. Then, you are free to devour some splendid middle class garbage. Now dig baby, dig." Ed cawed.

So, I dug and I dug and I dug. And I pulled and I pulled and I pulled and finally, low and behold I was free!

CHAPTER 7

The Garbage Frenzy

"WELL, WHAT ARE YA waitin' for? Let's get this show on the road." Ed cawed.

"What show?" I asked, dirty and confused.

"The garbage show, ya num skull. Come on Stewy, follow me, I'll show ya what ta do." Ed flew over my head, then spread his wings and swooped up into the bright blue sky. Ed was right; his feathers were much more beautiful than his cousin the crow. They seemed to shimmer and glow bright greenish blue in the sunlight.

I tried to follow Ed, but every time I took a few steps I would get entangled in my leash and the stake would get stuck in the grass and pull me to a screeching halt.

"Wait up Ed!" I yelled.

Ed turned around in the air, flew back to me and said, "Stewart my friend, this is never gonna work. I don't normally do this, but I'm gonna give you a hand. It's a good thing I have powerful wings and a strong beak."

Ed picked up my leash and led me out of our yard to the nearest neighbor's garbage can.

"Actually Stewart, this crazy contraption might just work out in our favor." Ed said as he swung the stake back and forth in front of the garbage can. He let go of it on the third swing and it crashed into the can, spilling the contents onto the sidewalk. "Bingo! Ladies and gentlemen, we got ourselves a winner." Ed hopped into the messy garbage and began poking around. "Now, Stewart, there's a method to dumpster divin' and I'm a gonna teach ya what it is. You, my canine friend, are lucky, because you have the power of smell."

"The power of what?" I asked.

"The power of smell my friend, the power of smell. You can take one big whiff of this mess and let us know whether or not it's worthy of bein' eatin'. Now breathe in real slow and take a big whiff."

I took a big sniff of the garbage.

"So, what da ya smell?"

"Well, I smell something sweet; kind of like the way Katie smelled in my dream. I also smell something that kind of stinks, and maybe a little bit of meat."

"There ya go my friend, the power of smell. We may have hit the jackpot on this one."

Ed began tearing through the garbage bag with his magnificent, long beak. That sucker was powerful and sharp.

"Oh yes, we hit the mother lode on this one Stewart. Check this out; roast beef, chicken pot pie, and pancakes and syrup. I'm not supposed to eat chicken, because the chicken is also my cousin. If you don't tell, I won't tell."

I dug into the delicious mess enjoying every bite. The pancakes and syrup tasted like Katie's hands did that first day I met her. So this is what human food tasted like? It was delicious! Why had I been eating puppy chow all this time? Human food was much tastier.

"Okay Stewart, time ta move on."

Ed picked up my leash and led me to the next house. He performed the same task as before, swinging my stake three times then releasing it into the garbage can. Again, the can tipped over and the contents spilled onto the sidewalk. I used the power of my nose and inhaled a horrible stench.

"Poopy diaper, poopy diaper alert!" Ed squawked. "Even a magpie can detect that smell."

"What the heck is a poopy diaper?"

"Oh Stewart, I forget you're just a pup. You must not have any little baby humans livin' with ya.

"Katie and Cooper are six and nine. What are babies?" I asked.

"Babies are human puppies. Babies are a pain in the butt. All they do is eat, cry and poop into these smelly plastic things that humans call diapers."

"Why don't babies just poop in the yard like we do?"

"Cuz they're not nearly as smart as the two of us. Let's get the heck away from this baby stench and move on."

We spent the next several hours knocking over and digging through middle class garbage cans. I was beginning to get very full, but Ed insisted that we hit just one more. We ended up at the house right next door to the pink palace.

We should have stopped while we were ahead.

B.i.g. Huge Mistake

"HAROLD. IS THAT A PUPPY and a magpie in our garbage can?" Kristi's neighbor asked her husband.

"Well, look at that, Pam. It's almost as if they're working as a team. I saw them down the street at the Cox's house doing the same thing. Do you think they understand each other?"

"It's the darndest thing I have ever seen. Whose puppy is that, and what on earth is it dragging behind it?" Pam asked. "You two scat! Go on home!" Pam yelled at us.

"Looks like it dug up its leash," Harold said. "What do you think you're doing in my garbage?" He yelled from the porch.

I had a hard time looking up from my pot roast and mashed potatoes. They would have been scrumptious if it hadn't been for the coffee grounds and egg shells that were mixed in.

Pam marched out of her house in her pajamas. Why was she wearing her pajamas in the middle of the day? "Go on home, I mean it! You have made quite the mess."

I looked around for my partner in crime but Ed had flown the coop. It was just little old me standing there with my leash and stake in a big pile of garbage.

Uh-oh. Ed had led me astray and I was going to be in big trouble with both Kristi and Dan the Man. I turned to leave, but my stake got caught in her flower bed. I pulled as hard as I could; pulling up a bunch of bright red flowers.

"Now you've done it, you bad puppy, you ruined my flower bed." Pam yelled.

I tucked my nub between my legs and waddled off as fast I could go, dragging my stake behind me.

"Look at that Pam. It looks like a little spotted bear cub." Harold said as I made my escape. "A naughty little bear cub."

I had no idea how long I had been out and about knocking over garbage cans with Ed. I decided I had better end my garbage feeding frenzy. Besides, Ed was nowhere to be found. He had left me high and dry to fend for myself. Maybe he wasn't such a good friend after all. I had made a B.I.G. HUGE MISTAKE!

I did what any bad dog would do at this point. I dropped my head in shame, drug my stake to the front porch and waited for my humans to come home. I really hoped that Kristi would be the first one home and not Dan the Man.

No such luck. Dan the Man pulled into the driveway about an hour later. "What in the heck?" I heard him say as he got out of his big white construction truck.

Luckily, Katie and Cooper were with him.

"Stewy Baby, what in the world have you done?" Katie asked as she came running towards me. "See Coop, I told you she didn't like being tied to the stake."

"That's awesome! It looks like she dug it up." Cooper said

"Well Stewart, it looks like Kristi's little plan to keep you outside in the sun today didn't quite work out." Dan looked mad, but not as mad as I thought he would be. "Let's take this darn collar and stake off of you and see what kind of damage you did to our backyard."

As Dan removed my collar, I licked his dirty construction hand to show him how much I appreciated him rescuing me from my blasted stake.

"Poor Stewy, poor, poor Stewy. You were all alone and afraid, weren't you Baby Girl?" Katie said as she picked me up.

"You're not off the hook yet. Let's see what you did to the backyard first." Dan said to me.

We were met halfway to the backyard by a grinning Cooper. "Dad, come check out this ginormous hole that Stewy dug up."

"Holy cow, you dug this hole all by yourself?" Dan asked me as he walked towards my ginormous hole.

(Well, I had a little help from Ed the Magpie. It was actually his idea). I wanted to respond to Dan.

"Look Daddy, we could fill the hole with water and Mommy could have the swimming pool that she's always wanted." Katie said jumping into the muddy hole and getting her pretty pink dress and shoes all dirty. Cooper joined her and they seemed to be having quite a good time in my new swimming hole.

"Guys, you better get out of there, we don't need to make it any bigger than it already is." Dan the man said to the kids. "I can't believe a little puppy like you, could dig a hole this big. What in

the world are we going to do with you?"
Dan asked me.

I barked to let him know that I didn't
know what in the heck they were going to
do with me, but I didn't want to be tied to
that stake ever again. Just to make sure he
knew exactly how I felt about the situation,
I gathered the stake in my mouth, dropped
it in the big hole and began to bury it with
the dirt and grass that I had dug up.

"Look Daddy, look! She's burying
her leash!" Katie pointed at me and
started laughing.

"Well I'll be darned. I believe you
now Katie, I think she does understand
humans." Dan said.

I barked again and ran around in circles
over my buried enemy. I thought I was
home free, and off the hook when Pam the
neighbor came walking over. She was still
in her pajamas. I was really scared that she
would narc me out.

"Hi kids, hi Dan. Is this your dog?" Pajama Pam asked as she busily looked around the yard.

"Yes Pam, I'm afraid it is, but I'm not sure that she's staying. What's up?"

"Hi Pam, I like your jammies. This is Stewy Baby, she's our new smart dog. She is staying. Daddy just doesn't know it yet." Katie babbled.

I barked at Pam and waddled over to her. I was begging her not to tell Dan about the garbage.

"Well hello there Stewy Baby. You were a busy puppy today weren't you?" Pam asked.

"Yeah, she was busy alright. Did you see the hole she dug to get herself free?" Cooper asked proudly.

"Well no, I didn't see the hole, but I saw him dragging the stake behind him all over the neighborhood." Pam said.

"Oh no, I was hoping she stayed put. She was waiting for us on the porch when we got home." Dan said.

"Yes well, it seems he had quite the adventure today. He and a magpie were seen all over the neighborhood getting into neighbor's garbage cans." Pam said laughing despite herself.

"I knew she would make a friend today!" Katie said.

"A magpie? What in the world? Stewarttttttt, were you a garbage dog?" Dan growled scolding me. He looked up at Pajama Pam. "I saw a lot of garbage cans knocked over, and wondered who had made the big mess. I'm so sorry Pam, we'll clean it up for you."

"No worries." Pajama Pam said. "Harold already took care of that. We just couldn't figure out who this little bear cub belonged to."

"Unfortunately, she is all ours." Dan said.

"Well, he certainly is cute, even if he is a garbage dog." Pam said.

"Silly Pam, she's a girl," Katie pointed out.

"How on earth did you come up with a name like Stewy for a girl?" Pajama Pam asked.

"Katie and I named her," Cooper said proudly. "Her full name is Stewart-Duke Anna-Belle Campbell. It's a cowboy-princess name."

"Oh my, yes. That explains a lot. Well Dan, I hate to be the bearer of bad news but she also pooped in Mrs. Camp's yard. I saw her do it myself and old Mrs. Camp was not happy about it," Pam tattled.

Once again, they were talking about me like I wasn't even there. It was bad enough that they were talking about whether I was a boy or a girl, they had to talk about my poop as well. Is nothing private?

"It looks like we scored points with all the neighbors today." Dan said.

"Yes, well it looks like you did Dan. I thought she ruined my flower bed, but Harold planted them again and they're good as new. It looks like a fence might be in your future." Pajama Pam said.

"Don't worry Dad, I'll help you build it," Cooper said.

"And I can help you pay for it; I have $.76 cents in my piggy bank." Katie said proudly.

"I'm really sorry for all the trouble Stewy caused you, Pam. A fence really wasn't in our budget this month. I don't think we're keeping her. "

What? Not keeping me? They have to keep me. This is where I belong, with my new family.

"Daddy, we have to keep her." Katie had scooped me up in her arms, a small tear rolled down her cheek and I gently licked it off. "We love each other."

"What do you think about a good neighbor fence?" Pam asked. "They are pleasant to look at. I was just talking with old Mrs. Camp and we decided we both need a fence. If you build it, we'll pay for it."

I squirmed out of Katie's arms and waddled over to Pajama Pam. I sat at her feet and whined. She kneeled down and gave me a nice pat. Then, I waddled over to Dan the Man. I bowed my head and lay at his feet.

"She's saying she's sorry, aren't you Stewy Baby?" Katie asked.

I barked to answer (yes).

"I can't say I feel like a good neighbor at the moment, but I think a good neighbor fence is a fine idea. Thanks Pam. Until it's built, we'll keep this puppy dog in a crate, so she doesn't cause any more trouble.

Come on kids, let's go clean up the neighborhood and say our apologies."

"Thank you Daddy." Katie walked over to Dan the Man and wrapped her small little hand in his.

I breathed out a big sigh of relief. Kristi was right. Dan the Man's bark was worse than his bite.

One Big Stinky Family

"HI GUYS I'M HOME!" Kristi said as she bounded through the front door.

Dan the Man and I were sitting on the pink living room floor eating popcorn and watching football.

"Well, it looks like the two of you have become good friends!" Kristi said. She walked over and kissed us both on the heads.

"You might say we bonded today." Dan said.

"Really? I knew you would! Where are the kids?"

"Mommy!" The kids came running down the stairs and gave Kristi a big hug.

"Mommy, Stewy Baby made a friend today. I told you she would." Katie said.

"She did, did she? Was she still out in the backyard tied to her stake? Dan, did you see the contraption Cooper and I rigged up for her?" Kristi asked proudly.

"Oh yes, I saw it, only I don't think I saw it the way you rigged it up." Dan said.

"What do you mean? Did she wrap herself around the tree? I was afraid of that…"

"Mom," Cooper interrupted "Stewy escaped from our contraption."

"What do you mean? How?"

"She dug the whole sucker up; you should have seen the huge hole in the backyard." Cooper said.

"Yeah Mommy," Katie continued "we wanted to put water in it and make a swimming pool for you…"

"But Stewy hated that leash so much she dropped it in the hole and buried it with dirt." Cooper finished.

I was rolling around on the pink carpet trying to ignore the fact that everyone was talking about my bad dog garbage day.

"She buried it? In the hole that she dug up?" Kristi said in amazement.

"Yes, in the hole that she dug up." Dan said.

"I told you we picked the smartest one Mommy." Katie said as she rubbed my big fat garbage gut. I was still paying dearly for my middle class garbage frenzy.

"What's that horrible smell?" Kristi asked, plugging her nose.

"Oh, that would be your garbage dog. It seems that eating garbage gives her a bad case of the wind." Dan said.

"She ate garbage?" Kristi asked Dan. "You ate garbage?" Kristi asked me.

"Yep, she ate garbage alright!" Cooper said. "We had to go around the neighborhood and clean up all the knocked over garbage cans."

"It was really gross and stinky. I got pudding all over my pink shoes." Katie said. "Then Daddy made us knock on the neighbors' door and introduce Stewy and apologize. Coop didn't want to talk and Stewy can't so I talked for all three of us."

"Yes, it seems that our puppy dog went on quite the adventure today. She and a magpie were wreaking havoc all over the neighborhood." Dan said.

"A magpie? You mean that black and white bird that's been hanging around in the backyard?" Kristi asked.

"Yep, that's Stewy's new friend, except she's kind of mad at him right now." Katie said.

I was still mad at Ed. I definitely wouldn't call him a friend.

Dan told Kristi the conversation that he had with Pajama Pam. Kristi just shook her head back and forth in amazement.

"And you're still smiling after everything she did?" Kristi asked Dan.

"Any mutt that is smart enough to dig up its entrapment, and bury it has my respect. Am I happy we have a big brown spot in our yard? No. Am I happy that half of our neighbors are angry with us because she ate their garbage and pooped in their yards? No. Am I happy that I have to build a fence? No. But, I do kind of like this mutt. She's smart, maybe a little too smart for her own good. This one is going to give us a run for our money." Dan smiled.

"Back up to the part about the fence," Kristi said. "You're building a fence?"

"Yep, Dad and I are building a fence next weekend," Cooper said.

"It's called a great neighbor fence, because we are great neighbors," Katie replied.

"It's called a good neighbor fence, Katie, and Dad said we're not good neighbors because Stewy got in everyone's garbage." Cooper corrected.

"That was before we cleaned up everyone's garbage for them, and said we were sorry. I'm pretty sure we're great neighbors again." Katie said.

"Let this be a lesson for all of us. Pets take work. You don't just buy one on a whim before you have everything in place." Dan said.

"Yes Daddy, but aren't you happy we have her?" Katie said. "You have to admit she is cute and smart and……"

"And stinky!" Cooper said as I let another one rip.

"Yes, I'm happy we have her." Dan said as he plugged his nose. "Katie Bug, you dreamed about the right one and you did well in choosing her."

We sat on the floor and finished the bowl of popcorn together, just one big stinky, happy family. Even Spud came over and joined us. He still gave me the stink eye, but it appeared to be a little less threatening. If I could win Dan the man over, anything was possible.

Yes, I dreamed about the right one – the red headed girl that smelled like maple syrup. I was sure that we would have great adventures together in our cozy pink palace!

Printed in the USA
CPSIA information can be obtained
at www.ICGtesting.com
BVHW010918310823
668996BV00004B/4